Lee Aucoin, *Creative Director*
Jamey Acosta, *Senior Editor*
Heidi Fiedler, *Editor*
Produced and designed by
Denise Ryan & Associates
Illustration © Samantha Paxton
Rachelle Cracchiolo, *Publisher*

Teacher Created Materials
5301 Oceanus Drive
Huntington Beach, CA 92649-1030
http://www.tcmpub.com
Paperback: ISBN: 978-1-4333-5458-8
Library Binding: ISBN: 978-1-4807-1137-2
© 2014 Teacher Created Materials

Zoo Hullabaloo
WITHDRAWN

Written by Sophie Valentine
Illustrated by Samantha Paxton

When I went to the zoo, the noise
was a riot!

2

There wasn't an animal there
that was quiet.

twitter

twitter

I walked past the birds

4

and then the raccoons.

I crept past the lions

and then the baboons.

7

I ran past the wolves

growl

growl

and the tigers, too.

9

I skipped past the camels

and even the gnu.

Then, it was quiet. So I stopped
for a while and smiled up at
the crocodile!